D1715744

WHEN the RAINS CAME

Dancer

Delmar Johnnie Seletze'

"Dancer" is the first in a series of five paintings that depict the artist's experiences as a Salish longhouse spirit dancer.

Inspired both by dreams and past experiences, "Dancer" portrays the artist's inner quest for meaning in receiving his Native name Seletze' and as a longhouse dancer. The larger character represents the past, a vital element in the quest, and wears ceremonial paddles, scratcher, black face, and feathered headdress, a family tradition. The small character symbolizes the artist looking out from the past in search of his new identity. This character also represents his search for a path that will incorporate the ways of the longhouse into his daily life.

WHEN the RAINS CAME

AND OTHER LEGENDS OF THE SALISH PEOPLE

as told to Dolby Bevan Turner
illustrated by D. Johnnie Seletze´

Orca Book Publishers

Canadian Cataloguing in Publication Data
Turner, Dolby, 1910–
    When the rains came and other legends
of the Salish People

    ISBN 0-920501-87-7
    1. Coast Salish Indians—Legends.   2.
Indians of North America—British Columbia—
Vancouver Island—Legends.   I. Seletze',
Delmar Johnnie.   II. Title.
E99.S21T87 1992   398.2'089'979   C92-09616-3

Publication assistance provided by The Canada Council

Cover design by Susan Fergusson
Illustrations by D. Johnnie Seletze'

Orca Book Publishers
P.O. Box 5626, Station B
Victoria, BC V8R 6S4
Canada

Printed and bound in Canada

I am grateful for their friendship, and honoured to have been told some of their legends. After these many years, I write of what they said, as closely as possible in their own words, so as to pass on intact the spirit of the stories I was entrusted with.

Their life was one of hardship, hunger, and privation; yet I never knew them to lose their self-esteem, nor to betray the beliefs they had been taught by the counsel of their elders.

If they in their time were able to hear the sounds of past battles and potlatches, is it not possible, now that they are a part of the past themselves, that they in turn can hear their people speaking today? How proud they would be of their Native lawyers as they discuss each legal issue with such wisdom, eloquence, and innate dignity!

The tide has turned; their Native dreams are at last becoming reality, and it is my hope that my old friends are aware of the high esteem in which their people are now held by all Canadians.

Dolby Bevan Turner

I appreciate and give thanks to Dolby Turner for writing this book. I appreciate her sharing the knowledge and words she heard from my ancestors. I have heard the stories before, but the way she begins the book with an introduction of my great-grandparents, Rosalie and Johnnie, makes the stories blossom with meaning and wonder for me. I feel most honoured to have done the illustrations for the stories.

Last but not least, I give thanks to Dolby for her respectfulness in that she requested and received from my people, Khenipsens and other Cowichans, permission to publish this book.

D. Johnnie Seletze'
July 1992

Contents

My father, Herbert Bevan, standing beside the "Welcome Pole," outside the longhouse on the Quamichan Reserve (circa 1908).

Introduction

A word of explanation is in order as to how I came to
have such an abiding interest in the affairs of the Native
people of Vancouver Island.

I was born and raised in the Cowichan Valley on Vancouver Island, where in 1906 my father, Herbert Bevan,
bought the four-hundred-acre property on the Maple Bay
Road, previously owned by a Mr. Skinner (who had been
a factor of the Hudson Bay Company). Dad named the
place Happy Hollow, and it was well named, for I spent
the happiest years of my young life there.

The land lay on the shores of Quamichan Lake; beyond it Mount Provost raised its heart-shaped crest into
the sky. According to the Salish legend, it was at the
base of this mountain that the first man came to earth.

Seventy-five years have passed since I had my first
contact with the Natives of Vancouver Island. I was about
six years old at the time. I had smelled smoke coming
from the direction of the playhouse that Dad had had

built for us children back in the woods behind our home. Afraid the little house was on fire, I ran up the trail to investigate. When I reached the clearing I saw a small cook-fire burning and, nearby, a strange, dark-skinned woman sitting on a log, a baby in her arms.

Stopping in my tracks, I stared at her. Had I come face to face with a big black bear, I could not have been more terrified. To my amazement, the woman half turned away and, lifting her arm as though to ward me off, said: "Go 'way—me scared."

No one had thought to tell me that Dad had hired some of the Natives to cut wood, and the woman was the wife of one of these men. Today, I look back in wonder; a grown woman afraid of a child? It was not until years later, after we had sold Happy Hollow and moved to Green Point, located at the foot of Mount Tzouhalem across from Cowichan Bay, that I learned of the white man's injustice to the Natives.

As our relations with the Salish people of the neighbouring Khenipsen Village grew into a true and lasting friendship, I began to ask about their traditions. Although they were at first reticent about telling them to a non-Native, I was in time able to draw out and record a number of their "old-time stories."

Sadly, as the older generation passes on, much of their ancient folklore is being lost. It has been one of my ambitions to write down as much of this material with which they have entrusted me as possible.

I am under obligation to many kind friends who have been generous with their time and talent; their advice and encouragement has been invaluable and, in fact, without their help this book would not have seen the light of day.

Dr. Douglas Leechman, author of *Indian Summer, Esquimo Summer,* and other works, came to Canada in 1924 to work in the Division of Anthropolgy of the National Museum of Canada. After he retired to Victoria in the 1950s, Douglas read the early legends I had written, and was most generous with advice as to their manner of presentation.

Wilson Duff, director of the old British Columbia Provincial Museum and a longtime friend, was consistently supportive, and gave me the courage to continue writing.

Don Abbot of the Royal British Columbia Museum in Victoria has opened many doors to help me find the information needed to made these stories authentic.

Robin Skelton, author and founder of the creative writing program at the University of Victoria, recently retired, has given me priceless encouragement.

Abner Thorne, an elder and councilman of the Cowichan Native Band, and a wise and gentle man, has spent many hours with me, telling me the Salish words and how to spell them. He also took me to see his mother, Agnes Thorne, nee Norris, a charming and very alert lady of eighty-five years and one of the few remaining sources of their legends.

Randy Bouchard and Dorothy Kennedy have a massive collection of records about the Native people, both written and on tape, which they were so generous as to share with me.

Linda Vander Berg, B.Ed., M.A., ethno-historical researcher and representative of the Native people in their land claims, has made it possible for me to meet and make friends with the younger generation in Cowichan.

Last, but by no means least, Dr. Cecil Miles, who taught Spanish at the University of Victoria after his retirement from a long career with the United Nations. He has become a staunch friend and has worked tirelessly editing my copy and taking on the duties of manager and literary agent. That my dream has not died stillborn is largely due to Cecil's efforts on my behalf. Thank you, Cecil!

D.B.T.
Victoria, February 1992

Green Point, Cowichan Bay. A place of many moods (circa 1926).

Rendezvous at Green Point

Cowichan Bay's Green Point—what a wealth of memories flood through my mind as I write this. The sights and sounds come sharply into focus, and the intervening years drop away as though they had never been—I am young again, and I am there once more.

I can see the misty dawns and the waters of Cowichan Bay stretching away like a well-ironed sheet, a long strip of driftwood cross-stitched with seaweed embroidering the hem-line close to shore, the salmon rolling on the surface, porpoise-like, cutting a thin line through the still water, only to dive and leave no trace of their passing.

Green Point was a place of many moods. Some days it was so peaceful one could almost touch the stillness—time seemed to stop, as though not one tomorrow could ever change it. There were evenings when the harvest moon took over the sun's sky before daylight ended, its light so bright we could read by it.

Then again there were times when a gale from the east would come swooping over the Saanich hills, whipping the sea into a fury and driving the waves crashing on the beach below. I see again the grey fan of rain drifting towards us and, when it had passed, ravens waddling pigeon-toed through sky-reflecting puddles, their ink-black feathers glinting indigo in the sun.

Yet sometimes it was haunted, and the past came crowding in. Spirits made their presence known; knocks were heard on the ceiling. Several of our guests actually saw these manifestations; others could only hear the beat of the drums, and voices chanting. Still others heard nothing.

We attributed these psychic phenomena to the old Chief Tzouhalem, for our cottage was built on the site of his longhouse. Later, when I discussed the strange happenings with the Natives, they first pretended to know nothing about them, but eventually one of them, Danny Thomas, admitted that such things were commonplace with his people; he only found it unusual that we should see and hear them as they did.

It was in 1926 that my family first rented Green Point. Then in 1929 we bought the 120 acres of land that lay across from Cowichan Bay along the foot of Mount Tzouhalem. To our left, the mountain sloped gently at first, then rose in sheer rock walls abruptly to the sky. On our right, the Cowichan River flowed the length of our land, ending its winding forty-mile journey from Lake Cowichan and spilling into the sea at the Point, where the waters of Cowichan Bay curved around our front door.

In order to reach our isolated haven, we had to drive over a long, narrow dike, then follow the deeply rutted track that served as a road through the Khenipsen village, separating the houses on the left from the grassy incline which sloped down to the still backwater that formed a safe harbour for the Natives' dugout canoes.

The first house belonged to Peter Jack. He was chief then, and the only one to own a two-storey building, which looked as though it had been transplanted from a city suburb, and, like a child adopted from some alien land, it remained a foreigner in the village.

The old longhouse came next. Wide cedar planks ran vertically from the ground to the great beams supporting the split shake roof. There was a single window facing the road, and two barn-like doors with a smaller one cut into one frame. Left open in the warm weather, these allowed a shaft of sun into the cavernous interior. It was truly a "long house"—more than ninety feet long and forty feet wide. Deep shelves round the walls on the lower levels served as sleeping platforms, while others of diminishing sizes slanted up in steps. During a dance, every inch would be crowded with guests sitting hip to hip, like rows of sparrows looking down on the performers leaping around the great fires.

On the ridge above the longhouse was a tall monument to Chief Tolpaymault. A plaque on the base declared that he had visited King Edward in England in 1909, and that he had been entertained by the governor general in Ottawa.

From the village the road wound on, skirting the clearing to the right beyond the entrance to the backwater. Part field, part bog, it belonged neither to land nor sea; winter tides held a half-year lease which gradually, grudgingly, they yielded to the sun's ever-increasing warmth. Then the clumps of coarse grass grew thick and green as the sea receded, allowing summer to claim the land for a meadow.

Beyond this, and high above, a huddle of homes clung to the contour of a rocky outcrop which backed onto the river. A well-worn footpath, dusty in summer and slippery-wet in winter, snaked to the top, in and out between the houses, which were clad in cedar planks or shingles, all mellowed to a soft, silver grey.

Rosalie, an elderly woman, and her husband Johnnie also had their home on the knoll. They were unusual in that they were of the few who had not abandoned their Salish name, Seletze'. Then came the homes of Danny Thomas, Johnnie Page, and several other families. I owe it to these gentle people, with whom we became friends, that I was able to listen to, and now record, some small part of their ancient folklore.

The dead of Khenipsen were buried on the far side of the promontory, in a glade where the ground sloped gently towards the river. They lay beneath a cathedral of trees so large and tall that the sun peered down at them through slats of interwoven branches. At night moonlight silvered the darkness and softly touched the graves. Sadly, so many children were buried there. Most had died of tuberculosis—not even the medicine man with all his magic could banish that slow, relentless reaper of their young.

The burial ground marked the beginning of our land. Beyond it, the road crossed over a planked bridge and then clambered up the side of the hill, which seemingly only a goat could negotiate. Finally, at the top, the land spread out and the road slid down into the flat field known as Green Point. It was here that the idea of writing down this medley of mythical legends of the Salish people was conceived.

Rosalie and Johnnie Seletze' sitting outside their home at Khenipsen (circa 1927).

Rosalie and Johnnie Seletze'

As I have said, Rosalie and her "old man" Johnnie lived in the last house on the bluff, perched high on the knoll overlooking the Cowichan River into which at low tide she would drop a bucket tied to a rope and haul up fresh water for her daily needs.

Their one-room home was always miraculously neat and tidy. It was furnished with a cast-iron stove, a white-painted wrought-iron double bed with brass knobs, a kitchen table covered with a length of gaily patterned oilcloth, two upright chairs, and an old rocker. Chipped enamel pots hung from nails driven into the wall behind the stove, and along another wall were shelves which held a great variety of household goods.

I once asked Rosalie how she managed to keep her home so uncluttered when she had so little space to put things.

"Oh—that no trouble," she explained with a shrug. "We don' got much." She pointed to a row of baskets on the floor, some stacked three high. "I keep things Indian way."

There was a great variety of these lovely baskets, woven in all sizes and designs, in which were stored sheep fleece and balls of wool, carded and spun, ready to be knitted into one of her much-prized Cowichan sweaters, one of which is still worn by a member of my family—granted, it is not as fleecy as it was sixty years ago, but it is still a fine sweater. Some of the Natives used to dye their wool, but never Rosalie. She would only use the natural shades of white, grey, and brown, and the hard-to-come-by black when she could get it.

Tree fungi were placed here and there around the room, some of which had been painted red. When I asked her why she had them, she said, "Oh, them things. Them's good, keep all-a bad spirits away."

"Is there a reason for painting them?" I wanted to know.

"That bring good luck, lotsa good luck. I make paint from red stone. Indian paint—lotsa hard work, but you do that, no bad thing come to your home."

"Well, if that's the case, Rosalie, I'm going to find a fungus for my home; we all need to keep the evil spirits away."

"You wait," she said, nodding her head. "I give you something good." And, selecting a small basket, she lifted the lid and produced a thing about an inch long that looked like a mummified baby octopus.

"Ah, him too small. Here, you take two, that makes 'em strong," she said, handing them to me.

"Thank you, Rosalie, but what do I do with them?" I asked. "Are they good luck charms, too?"

"Ah, yes. Hold in your hand. Hold and make wish. You want man, you want money, whatever you want, you get."

I held them as she told me, and suddenly I felt them grow

warm and pulsing, like a faint heartbeat. "They feel alive!" I exclaimed. "What on earth are they?"

"That spirit come you quick," Rosalie said, smiling. "Them's roots from Indian wild potato. Long, long time ago we eat, before white man potato." Thanking her, I wrapped them in my hanky and put them in my purse.

Some days later, on my way into Duncan, I stopped at the village to ask Rosalie if she would knit me a sweater. As I pulled into the turnabout at the bottom of the dusty trail up to her home, I noticed the government nurse's car parked there. As I drew up alongside and parked, I saw Rosalie chasing the nurse down the path, swinging a deck mop and yelling as she ran after the fat woman, threatening her with the soggy weapon.

I had never before heard Rosalie shout, much less seen her move so fast. She was yelling, "You say I gotta marry my old man"—swoosh went the mop—"You tell me marry my old man or you no give medicine"—slosh—"You no come back"—swoosh.

Luckily, the nurse managed to stay a few feet ahead. Despite her considerable weight, she was agile, and with leaps and bounds reached the safety of her car, and with seconds to spare started the motor, slammed the door, and was off, every time-worn spring and bolt groaning in protest as she drove full-tilt along the narrow, rutted road.

I had a hard time to keep from laughing as I walked over to where Rosalie had skidded to a stop.

"What on earth was all that about? You scared the daylights out of that woman."

"Good—I fix her, that no-good nurse—she come back again, I fix her good."

Rosalie was obviously so angry and out of breath she couldn't talk, so I waited a while before asking again, "What has she done to upset you like this? Do tell me."

Breathing heavily and using her mop as a staff, Rosalie stood shaking her head from side to side as her eyes followed the nurse's car until it disappeared behind the brush at the far end of the dyke. Only then did she turn to me, saying, "That no-good nurse—she tell me I gotta marry my old man. I gotta marry him in her church, or she no give medicine."

Speaking more slowly, she added, "I've been married to my old man maybe sixty years. Married our own way—long, long time ago, when I was just a young girl. Now that no-good nurse, she say I gotta marry him her way. How she go talk—she got no husband."

I patted her shoulder in an attempt to calm her down saying, "Don't worry, Rosalie, I am sure you are just as much married as anyone could be. But tell me, what seems to be wrong with Johnnie?"

Her eyes filled with tears, and thumping her chest, she said, "I don't know, he get bad pain here—maybe he go die."

"I'm on my way into town. How would it be if I asked our doctor to come and see Johnnie? Our doctor is a good man and I'm sure he'll take care of him."

"Oh, thank you—maybe he make 'em better again," she said, her face brightening with hope. "You come see my old man. I make tea—you come now." She led the way up the trail, the damp mop swinging its stringy head over her shoulder until we reached her home. There she hung it over a nail outside the door.

Following her inside, I saw Johnnie sitting in the rocker, looking so frail I felt he must have passed his curve of time *and was fast sliding down the far side.*

While Rosalie went to the stove and poked the fire, filled the kettle with water from a galvanized bucket, and put it on to boil, I told Johnnie about the nurse's hasty departure and of the plan to have my family doctor come to see him. He said nothing, but with a slight smile nodded in agreement.

The three of us sat quietly, saying little as we drank our tea. By the time we had finished, Rosalie had relaxed. She looked at me and began to smile; then, turning to Johnnie, a broad grin spread across her face as she said to him, "That no-good nurse—she don't know nothin', we don' need her, ah."

Johnnie had always been a man of few words, and his chuckle as he began to rock said everything. Watching Rosalie's happy face and thinking of the nurse's dash for safety, I started to laugh. When Johnnie's chuckle deepened, my friend, too, began to shake with laughter until her ample frame was heaving up and down.

After the merriment had subsided, we sat quietly. The sun was shining on the water, causing ripples of light to come through the window and dance around the room. After a while she looked at me, then pointed to Johnnie, and I saw he was fast asleep, slumped in the rocking chair, a smile still on his face. I half rose to leave, but Rosalie motioned for me to stay.

"You have been kind—I think you like to hear another of our legends?"

"I would love it," I answered. "But what about Johnnie? Wouldn't we wake him up if we talk?"

"No, he sleep like a baby. Now he know he get help, he no worry. You know the story about when the rains came?" she questioned.

"I haven't heard the one that comes from here. There are many versions of that story from all over the world, but each is different in its own way—please tell me yours."

And so Rosalie began to tell me the Salish version of the legend of the flood.

When the Rains Came

as told by Rosalie Seletze'

Back in the time when the people here saw the rains begin to pour down as they never had before, they said to each other, "It is good that we have all the salmon smoked and dried and safely stowed away."

And an old woman added, "It is good that the young girls gathered so many salmonberries and had time to crush and dry them into cakes before the rains began."

Another said, "Don't forget the women who took their digging sticks and brought us such a harvest of camas roots."

"We have no need to worry," a young brave said. "We have had rains before. It will stop soon—why are my people afraid?"

The chief rose to his feet, spread his arms wide, commanding silence, and addressed the gathering seated in the longhouse. Turning to the youth, he began to speak. "You, young man, are more foolish than brave. The rain has been falling week after week. The water has risen so high that all the houses will soon be flooded. We have to be sure our children are safe." He paused, and then continued, "I ask all the men who are able-bodied to go up into the hills and cut down cedar trees. Cut enough to make a raft so wide and long that our young ones can be floated to safety, and big enough to store the food they will need to last them until the waters go down."

Then he added, "When the trees are cut, you must skin off the outer bark and strip off the soft inner lining. Give it to the women to pound and oil, pound and oil, over and over again, until it is waterproof, before twisting it into a rope, long and strong enough to anchor the raft so that our children will not float away and be lost."

An elder asked, "Where will you tie the end of this rope?"

"There is a hole in a rock at the top of the mountain. When the time comes, tie it there and the raft will be secure."

By the time the chief finished speaking, the water was already inside the house. All the men rushed to do his bidding. Each worked until exhausted as they took turns to chop, then rest, then chop again, day after day.

And still the rains poured down, day after day, night after night, until all the houses were under water. Then everyone climbed the mountain, each carrying a child or storage baskets filled with food. Day after day they ascended higher until they reached the base of the rock cliff, where they could go no higher.

The raft was finished and afloat, the long, long rope was fastened to it, and the best climber, holding the other end, managed to scale the rock face and tie the rope through the hole the chief had told them about.

The elders now had the difficult task of choosing one young man and one young woman to go on the raft and look after the children. At last, all agreed on one sixteen-year-old who was wise for his years, strong and healthy. The girl chosen was one fifteen years old, who had recently become a mother.

The raft was loaded with baskets of food which were stored under a shelter of deer skins that would also serve to catch drinking water. Cedar mats were spread over the logs to prevent the little ones from slipping.

Last of all, the children were lifted onto the raft. Not one was left behind. Finally the young man and the young mother, her weeks-old baby in her arms, joined them. He carried two long poles to be used to fend against the rocky rise of the mountaintop, since if the wind should blow, the raft could be swept against it, weakening the cedar cords that held the logs together.

Those on the raft could see their elders standing on the last foothold of land. A few had climbed into trees to live a little longer as they watched the raft float higher and higher.

As the dull grey day faded into the blackness of night, not one of those left behind had cried out, nor shown fear or sorrow. They would live on through their children.

The rain kept falling, day and night, for weeks on end.

The young slept well through the first night, as children do, the young man and woman only in snatches, concerned for their charges. Then one morning they looked out and could see nothing but water; the last peak of Mount Tzouhalem was gone, and they were alone, floating on an endless ocean.

Day followed day, night followed night, until one morning the young man looked about him, rose up, and, stepping carefully between the slumbering children, went to where the young mother was sleeping. He touched her gently to awaken her and said, "Look up. I think the clouds have dried out. Does it not look less grey to you?"

And indeed, the sky seemed to have a soft glimmer of light, a thing she had not seen for weeks on end, and as she sat up she realized the rain no longer fell.

"How long?" she asked. "How long before we see land again? There is very little food left. How long before the children starve?" she asked again, unable to conceal her anxiety. "How long can we survive?"

Before the young man could reply, they saw something swimming towards them. When it came close, they discovered that it was a seal, carrying a salmon in its mouth. On reaching them, it raised itself up out of the water and dropped the fish onto the raft. From a scar on its back, the young man saw that this was the animal he had discovered as a pup laying on the beach, bleeding from a long gash. He had carefully picked it up, carried it back to his home, fed it, and nursed it back to health. The two had become inseparable until the pup became an adult. Then, although loath to leave its human companion, it found the call of nature too strong. One day it left to join a pod of seals, mate, and remain with its own kind.

The seal gave three sharp barks of joy at having found its friend, and the young brave on his part was so delighted that he dived into the water and hugged his boyhood playmate. They romped together for a long time, just as they had in the past, until the time came for the young man to climb back onto the raft and help feed the children.

The next morning the sun was shining, and from then on it continued to shine, day after day. The seal stayed nearby, bringing an endless supply of fish, and so they were saved from starvation.

It was one evening, when the sun was sinking below the horizon, that they caught their first glimpse of land in the form of a dark speck silhouetted against the sky. No one slept well that night, and excitement ran high. One of the older children was moved to say, "That must be the top of our mountain." Another, reluctant to hold such hope, answered, "It could be just a canoe that has floated up." And so they spoke until the young brave said, "Enough. Go to sleep—we shall know better in the morning." And so they slept for one more night.

When they awoke next morning, the object was still there, only larger. It was clearly no canoe. It was land at last; the waters were draining away, and sometime soon they would return home.

Each day the mountain became bigger, until the raft with its precious young was floating even with the base of the rock cliff where their elders had so willingly given their lives to save them.

Each day, as the waters receded, the young brave and the young woman would take hold of the two long poles and, using them as planned, fend off the snags and ledges, so keeping the raft floating free until at last it came to rest at the place where their homes had been before the rains came.

The seal stayed with them and continued to bring them fish until the young people were able to manage on their own. Then, and only then, did it leave and not return.

Johnnie was still sleeping when Rosalie had finished telling me the legend. I stood up, motioning her to follow me outside before saying anything, afraid my voice would disturb Johnnie's rest. As we stepped outside, I thanked her for telling me the Salish version of the flood.

One question had been building in my mind as she told me the story. In all the legends I had read or heard of, the survivors always somehow returned to dry land, but none had ever told what they found on their return. Even the Ark, when it landed on Mount Ararat, seems to have left people and animals stranded halfway down. I wanted to know what the children found when the raft came to rest, so I asked, "Were they any houses left, or did those young ones have to start again from nothing?"

"Ah no, the homes were still there, only there was lots of mud—took a long, long time to clean it out."

"Thank you, Rosalie," I said. "At last one version has an ending. That makes me feel good."

More than sixty years have passed since that day, but I can still see Rosalie as she looked then, standing straight with pride and dignity as she said good-bye to me. I have wondered many times since—whether it was our doctor's medicine, the red-painted fungi, the pulsing camas root, or just Rosalie's great love for her "old man" that kept him safely beside her for several more years?

Rosalie died in 1934, surviving Johnnie by only six months.

Danny Thomas heading for the fishing ground. He pauses as he rows past Green Point to speak to my sisters, Edie and Mary, and me (circa 1928).

Danny Thomas

The sun was high overhead as I walked through the village of
Khenipsen, my shadow bumping along beside me on the rutted road which wound between weatherworn houses on the
left and a grassy incline leading down to the long, narrow
backwater of the Cowichan River.

The tide was low, and the rushing waters of the river
could be heard singing beyond the ridge that forms the safe
harbour for the dug-out canoes, now pulled up and beached
below the owners' homes.

No one was about, only a small, friendly dog standing at
the doorway of the longhouse. Then I saw Danny Thomas
sitting on a log by the water's edge. He was leaning forward,
elbows resting on his widespread knees, working away at
something. As I walked towards him, I could see that he was
filing a copper fishing spoon, changing the Gibbs-Stewart
commercial shape into a design of his own (Danny was a fine
fisherman and was recognized as the most successful).

Intrigued, I moved closer and asked, "What are you doing—

and where are the rest of the people?"

"Everyone gone hop picking. I stay here, feed-em dogs and fix-em spoon catch-em lotsa salmon—they swim here pretty soon." Danny's first language was Salish.

"May I sit with you for a while, Danny?" I asked.

He raised his head, covered with a thatch of iron-grey hair, and looked at me through deep-sunken eyes; then a smile spread across his weather-beaten face and, nodding his head, he patted the log beside him, saying, "Long time, long time I no see you. You sit here."

The amenities having been disposed of, he methodically went on filing and bending his spoon. I sat there for quite some time as he continued working, and not a word was said. Once in a while he would stop and tie the spoon to a length of fishing line attached to the end of a pole, then he would drop it into the backwater and test its action by slowly drawing it back and forth.

"What is it you are trying to do?" I asked.

"See," he said. "Fool big fish."

The spoon was darting about in an odd manner, so I said, "It looks like a wounded trout, Danny. If I were a fish, I'd go for it!"

"That's right, big salmon see it, he think he catch easy dinner—but I catch big salmon, take home, fill empty belly— lotsa empty bellies."

After many more tries, more filing and bending, Danny had it working exactly as he wanted. Satisfied, he put the spoon aside and sat down with me, trying to ease the pain in his rheumatic hands by pressing them between his knees.

I don't know how old Danny was then; his face was

deeply creased and weatherworn, much like the cedar-planked longhouse behind us. There were heavy lines running to his full-lipped mouth, which was so large that when he smiled his face was almost split in two, the upper half lifting the high cheekbones so that his eyes almost disappeared. Danny was no beauty, but he was a dear old man, wise and gentle and full of the knowledge of his people's origins. Like the beget and begot of the white man's Bible, he could relate right back to his tribe's beginnings.

I had been trying for a long time to find him in the mood to tell me something of all this that he had locked in his head; today seemed too good an opportunity to pass by. So, ending a long silence, I turned to him and said, "You promised to tell me some of your old-time stories. Would you have time to tell me some today?"

"Tell old story . . . " He bent down and retied the bit of heavy fishing line he had substituted for a lace in his well-worn shoes. Then, looking towards the incoming tide at the mouth of the backwater, and noting the path of the sun so as to judge the time left before the evening fishing, he nodded and said, "We no speak about the things . . . but for you I tell story of the Stonehead People."

And so, without attempting to transcribe his dialect, here is Danny's version of the Legend of Kis-ack.

The Legend of Kis-ack and the Stonehead People

as told by Danny Thomas

Many long years ago a savage war-like tribe of Indians lived here at Khenipsen village. They were known as Stoneheads, and were feared all up and down the coast, and even far away on the mainland.

It was believed that their heads were made of stone because when they attacked some peaceful village, the defending braves were unable to wound a Stonehead, much less kill one. Their arrows would hit with a thump, bounce off, and fall on the ground, and any brave who got close enough to strike a blow with his club always found his weapon shattered with the first whack and, defenceless, he would be struck down and mercilessly slaughtered.

During one of the raids on a northern tribe, the Stonehead chief captured a beautiful young maiden. She was well treated and, unlike the other captured slaves who were often beaten and starved, she was allowed to live with the chief's family as one of his wives.

A year later, this slave gave birth to a girl child. As luck would have it, the baby took after her mother, having none of the ugliness of her Stonehead father. As the child grew to womanhood, she became even more beautiful than her mother. The old chief was proud to have such a lovely daughter and she became his favourite child.

Young braves tried in vain to win her, but she would have none of them. They would speak with her father, but the old chief would say, "Don't come to me, young man. My daughter will choose for herself."

This went on until his storage boxes were filled to overflowing with the rich gifts from the various suitors.

Each suitor presented his finest furs, ornaments, or carvings as a token of his worth, trying to impress the old chief, who would then thank each donor and pretend to listen sympathetically to the pleading and promises of what the young man would do if the Chief would only choose him.

"I shall see that your home has all the wood you can burn to keep you warm throughout the coldest winter," one would say.

"I am a great hunter. You will never have the need for food for your family if you will give me your daughter," another would offer.

The chief, his face stony and expressionless, heard them all and inwardly laughed to himself. He was the great chief. With so many slaves, would he worry about firewood, food, furs, fish, or any other need, great or small? Not he.

He had no intention of allowing his daughter to marry anyone, but he was greedy. Rich gifts pleased him and the eager young men amused him. Suitors who foolishly annoyed him by becoming too pressing met with fatal accidents. Others quickly learned to accept the chief's statement, "My daughter must choose for herself."

A few miles upriver from the Stonehead encampment of Khenipsen lay the old village of Comiakin, which was perhaps the oldest in all the land. Comiakin was built by the first people in the Cowichan Valley, and is still home to the descendants of the tribe who lived there at the time of this story.

The Comiakin men are handsome, but the chief's son was the most handsome, and as brave as he was strong.

Naturally, all the young Comiakin maidens tried every trick they could think of to catch his eye, but he knew what they were up to and would say to himself as he smiled a greeting, "Silly girl, you have spent so much time trying to make yourself pretty that there is none left in the day to do a woman's work. How useless you are!" Then he would go hunting or fishing, or to play football with the other young men of his village.

One day when the young man was tracking a cougar, the trail led him along the slope of Mount Tzouhalem. It was there that he caught his first glimpse of the daughter of the Stonehead chief. Many times he had heard of her grace and beauty, but he thought the young bucks were exaggerating. He watched as she gathered marsh grass from the riverbank, and it took him only a minute to decide that the cougar hunt could wait for another day. Silently making his way down the slope and out of the underbrush, he stood in the open, some distance away so as not to frighten her, and waited for her to notice him.

The girl took her time choosing each blade of grass, for each must be the right colour, length, and quality for the special baskets that she wove. She sang as she worked her way along the bank until, looking up, she saw the young man standing, smiling, a hand raised in the traditional friendly greeting.

Shyly, she returned his smile, and waited as he walked towards her. She noticed his expressive brown eyes, the straight, well-shaped nose, the firm but gentle smiling mouth showing his white, even teeth, and she wondered how a man could be so handsome.

"I am of the Comiakin band," he introduced himself.

"And I am of the Stonehead tribe," she replied.

"Many times I have heard of you. I find it hard to believe you are of the Stoneheads," he said with obvious admiration.

"My mother was from the north," she explained. "My father says I look very much like her. She died when I was a small child, so I don't remember her, only her gentleness."

"Please forgive my rudeness. I intended no insult to the chief, your father. It is only . . . " he finished off with an apologetic smile.

Seeing his embarrassment, she encouraged him to talk about himself. The afternoon passed as they talked companionably, sitting beneath a giant cedar by the edge of the river.

The sun set in a burst of glory and the tide, unnoticed, crept in, covering the land. The bright red sky was reflected across the waters of Cowichan Bay. They realized the day was ending and she was long overdue home.

Before they parted, they arranged to meet whenever possible, screened from curious eyes beneath the low weeping branches of a maple. They spent happy hours together each time, finding it harder and harder to say goodbye. Each meeting found the Comiakin brave becoming more in love with the Stonehead maiden and more determined to speak to her father. The day came when he said impatiently, "I will wait no longer. Look at me and tell me, do you want to be my wife?"

"You must know I do, more than anything. I am nothing without you. You carry my heart with you so that I am not alive when you are away."

"Then come with me now and I shall speak to your father of our love."

"My father has said many times that I must choose my own man," she said slowly, "but he can be cruel and I am afraid for you. He will change his mind when he finds that I would leave him."

"Is your father not a man of his word? Will he say one thing and do another? That is not the way of a chief. Come! We will go now. You have made your choice. I am not afraid."

Taking her by the hand, he led her into the Stonehead village. They entered the longhouse and he walked with her to the far end, where the chief was sitting on his high platform. The young man was brave, perhaps the most fearless young man of his day, but for the first time his courage almost failed him.

The chief appeared so formidable. His face showed

no smile of welcome, no expression at all. Had it not been that his eyes moved, any stranger might have thought he was looking at a face carved from stone.

"Great Chief," the young man said, standing straight and proud. "I have come to ask your permission to marry your daughter."

The old man didn't blink an eye, just stared at the young brave. He then looked at his daughter and asked, "How speak you?"

"I would choose this man for my husband. I wish it as much as he."

The old man was no fool. He realized he had trapped himself into a position where he would have to keep his promise. If he refused to allow the marriage he would lose face.

He did some quick thinking. His daughter's choice was the son of the powerful Comiakin chief who had long been an enemy of the Stoneheads. This marriage would make peace between the two tribes. If he could persuade the young couple to make their home at Khenipsen, he would not only keep the girl with him, he would also gain a mighty ally.

"Would you leave me in my old age?" he asked in a pathetic tone. "Who will care for me when I am ill?"

Acting the part of a broken-hearted father, he managed to shed a few tears. Holding up his hands, he counted off the various tasks which were her duties, until he ran out of fingers and ideas. He sat with both hands raised, palms out, looking like a carved figure on a totem pole.

He played his part so well that the young couple felt

sorry for him. Together they stepped back and held a whispered conversation and came to a decision.

"Would you allow this marriage," the young man offered, "if we lived here with you at Khenipsen?"

The chief slowly lowered his hands as if all objections were draining out of him.

"You would make this your home?" he asked, pretending surprise.

"And you, my daughter," turning to her, "do you agree?"

"Yes, Father. I will always be your daughter and care for you, and my man shall be as a son to you. He will bring much glory to our tribe, for he is greatly honoured by all for his skill and wisdom."

The old man was silent for a long time. Then, as though he had a difficult decision to make, he said, "Very well, you shall be married on the day of the full moon, two moons from now."

Runners bearing this news were sent off with invitations to all the important chiefs for a big potlatch in honour of the wedding. Great preparations were made. Countless fish were speared and many deer and elk killed by the hunters' arrows and carried back to the longhouse. Huge piles of logs were cut and stacked in readiness for the three enormous fires that would burn day and night down the centre of the big lodge.

At last, all was ready and the guests arrived. Some neighbouring tribes came by foot. Some arrived by canoes that carried forty or more people. Feasting lasted for three days. Dancers, wearing wooden masks carved in the likeness of animals or birds and dressed in highly decorated costumes, leaped around the fires. The re-sounding beat of the drums kept time to the chant of voices, rising and falling in unison. Exhausted dancers were led off to the side, to be replaced by fresh ones.

On the last day of the wedding festivities the young couple was led into the centre of the longhouse, and there, in front of all, declared as one, in accordance with the Indian custom.

The old chief was delighted to have his daughter and son-in-law live with him in the longhouse and led them to the section he had set aside for them. There, in the far corner, they would make their home.

Life was good to the young couple for several months, despite the chief's demands upon them. They were very attentive and fulfilled their promise of caring for him, and in so doing became so close that the chief would not allow others to be near him.

Many were the angry looks and gestures thrown their way by the children of his first woman. They felt set aside and deeply resented the favours shown to his daughter by a slave and her man.

The council held many meetings with the Medicine Man, planning to cast a spell and so rid themselves of the upstarts. But the spell must have been misdirected, for it was the old chief who became ill of a sickness that none of the Medicine Man's magic could cure, and he died.

A short time later the Stonehead braves openly turned against the bridegroom. Not only were they jealous of his superior skills in hunting and fishing with spears, bows, and arrows (and even in sport he always did best), but each rejected suitor was also furious that he had won the girl each had wanted for himself. They never missed a chance to make his life as miserable as possible. One day, in exasperation, the Comiakin brave turned on one tormentor, wrestled him to the ground, and held him there. Within seconds the rest of the young bucks, using the attack as an excuse, leapt upon their hated rival and tore him limb from limb. Severing his head, they stuck it onto a pole and displayed it in front of the longhouse where the young wife would find it on her return from berry picking. Had the old chief been alive, they would not have dared to harm his son-in-law, for he would have protected his daughter's man.

The heartbroken widow was soon to become a mother. One night, as she lay in the corner of the longhouse, she overheard the Medicine Man and her cousins planning to kill her baby if it were a boy.

Terrified for the safety of her child, she pretended she hadn't overheard them plotting. Shortly before the baby was due to be born, she gathered together the items she had made for the child: a carrying basket padded with dry moss, furs to wrap it in, and, most important, a length of soft sinew to tie off the cord that bound them together, and last, the wide band she had woven to cover the wound. Then she moved into the women's birthing house at the edge of the forest, from which she hoped to escape if she should have a son.

She made the change just in time, for her hour had come. The child was well on its way when the Medicine Man and a cousin's mother entered, saying, "We have come to keep you company—you must be lonely."

"You are kind, but I feel sleepy and look forward to a quiet night."

It was dark in the cabin so they couldn't see her clearly, and although they were suspicious, they left, muttering to themselves.

A short time later the Medicine Man returned and said, "I thought I heard you moan and have come to help you."

"Thank you," she replied, in as normal a voice as she could manage. "The baby is in no hurry—perhaps tomorrow. The baby seems to have changed its mind."

"That sometimes happens with a firstborn," said the Medicine Man, believing her story, "but it could start again at any time, so I shall sit with you."

"No, leave me," the desperate girl ordered. "Go back and tell everyone to leave me alone. I wish to sleep. Now go."

Even the Medicine Man had to obey the daughter of a chief, and so, turning, he stamped out of the cabin in a rage.

The child was born a short time later, and, as she held her baby in her arms, she sent out an urgent prayer for help to Saghalie-Tyee (the Great Spirit), for the baby was a man child.

Working quickly, she tied off the cord, bit it free, and then wrapped the bellyband firmly around him, swaddling him tightly so as to completely conceal the physical proof that the baby was a boy.

Night had fallen and it was pitch-dark when the Medicine Man, who could wait no longer, returned to the cabin and found the young mother holding her sleeping child in her arms.

"So, it is over," he said. "Do you have a man or a woman child?"

"I have a daughter. Now please go and let me rest."

"I want to hold her," he ordered. Reaching out, he took the child and ran his hand over its body, searching, but could feel no evidence of manhood. Saghalie-Tyee must have heard the daughter's desperate prayer, for the evil man left.

Waiting until she could hear the Medicine Man talking in the longhouse and sensing that the time was right, the new mother placed her son in the carrying basket, covered him with furs, and stealthily left the cabin, disappearing into the forest. Moving silently so as not to alert the wicked plotters, she fled through the night until she had placed a safe distance between herself and the village of the Stoneheads.

By the first light of dawn she was able to see her son clearly for the first time, and as she held him to her she cried with gratitude, for the boy was the image of his father, and she named him Kis-ack. The exhausted girl sent another prayer to the Great Power, asking for protection and the strength and the wisdom she would need to defend her son from the dangers that would beset him.

At last she could rest. Sleeping fitfully, she considered what she must do. Her husband's people would be delighted to welcome her and the only child of the chief's eldest son, but if she turned to them for shelter, that would be the first place the Stoneheads would seek them out. This would mean war, and they would inevitably kill not only her son, but all her husband's tribe. It was important, therefore, that she keep hidden until her son was a man. When he was grown, he would avenge his father's murder.

On the morning of the second day she happened upon a lovely waterway, now known as the outlet of Quamichan Lake, and it was here she decided to make their home. Choosing a site beside the stream, just below the waterfall where the bank was soft and sandy, she managed to hollow out a cave large enough for them to live in. She fashioned a soft, comfortable bed of cedar bark, which she had pounded between two rocks until it was as light and pliable as duck down.

Night and morning she carried the child to a pool below the falls and ritually bathed him, cleansing him of all things evil, so that he might grow to be as strong and courageous as his father.

The years passed until his sixth summer, when the young brave was big enough to learn to use a bow and arrow. He hadn't yet the strength to use a full-sized hunting bow, but she made her son a small one and encouraged him to bring little birds to her as proof that he was learning. She would carefully preserve each bird skin. When he was grown, she would make him a magic coat by joining the skins together.

Despite her loneliness, she was happy. Her son grew to be a fine boy. They had long talks in the quiet hours of the evening, and Kis-ack loved best to hear about his father.

"Why doesn't my father come to see us?" he asked one day.

"He can't. Many moons must pass before I can tell you the full story. When you have reached manhood, then, my son, I shall tell you."

"When I am ten?"

"No, older."

"When I am fifteen?"

"No, more than that."

"When I am eighteen?"

"Yes, my son. Then I shall tell you why he can't be with us."

For the first time Kis-ack saw his mother cry. She wept as though her heart would break.

When she could control her sobs, she said, "Always remember to stay well hidden when strangers pass near. Some might be friends, others would harm you."

———

Kis-ack became skilled in magic. This came down to him from his mother's family. Daily he practised, becoming ever more proficient, and by his eighth summer he found he could understand the birds, and he would talk with them. Many times they warned him of danger when men were approaching, because they could see them long before Kis-ack did, and he was never discovered.

Kis-ack's mother was greatly pleased with him, and always urged him on to develop his magic powers, never failing to let him know how much she loved him. The bond between the two grew ever stronger.

In the spring of his fourteenth year his mother said, "You are now old enough to travel to more distant places. You must hunt for bigger game, and in your travels you will discover new magic; soon you will be a man, and men must be fearless hunters." She hesitated and then, looking at her son, she smiled her love. "Just as women must learn to wait with faith for their return."

With a heavy heart she watched him walk away the next morning, but she knew that only by sending him off to do a man's work could he grow to become the great fighter he must be if he was to right the wrong done by the Stoneheads, and accomplish all she had dreamed for him. It was this dream that had given her the courage to survive through those long, lonely years.

From that day on, Kis-ack hunted further afield. By his seventeenth summer he had reached his full strength and sometimes was away for several days and nights. One day he came to a lake that stretched far off into the distance (now known as Lake Cowichan). He saw a large herd of elk, some with enormous antlers. Choosing a big buck, he crept silently upwind to within shooting distance and, placing a flint-headed arrow in his bow, took aim and let fly. The great beast fell to the ground, mortally wounded.

This was the first time Kis-ack had seen an elk so close, and as he approached it he was amazed to find out how large it was. He now had to solve the problem of getting it home.

Growing beside the lake was a grove of alder saplings. Kis-ack cut two sturdy branches and made a long Y-shaped sled. He skinned the carcass and fastened the elk hide firmly to the frame, then he loaded the meat on it. Tying the antlers on top, he had little difficulty dragging it along the well-worn game trails. But when he came to rocky outcrops, it took all his strength to keep moving. At sundown he at last reached home.

"What fine tools you will make of these horns," his mother said. "And what fine coverings we shall make from this large hide."

"And what a fine dinner we shall have tonight," Kis-ack said. "While you cook, I shall bathe in the pool."

"Go, my son. Wash the tiredness out of you. I shall call you when it is time to eat."

But it was he who called, "Mother, come—I want you to see my magic." As she stepped from the cave to look, Kis-ack rubbed his skin with a piece of fir bark until he bled, then threw the bark into the water. The stream became a glittering mass of silver trout where there had been none before.

The winter passed, and Kis-ack reached the summer of his eighteenth year. He had grown to his full stature, and his mother knew she must now reveal the secret she had kept locked away in her heart for so long. When her son returned from bathing one evening, she called to him, "Come, sit with me. The time has come to answer the questions you have asked."

"About my father?" Kis-ack asked eagerly, noting her serious expression.

"Yes, about your father and the brutal Stoneheads."

She began slowly, and talked far into the night. Not once did Kis-ack interrupt. She told him of the cold-blooded way the Stoneheads had slain his father, and how they had planned to kill him also at his birth.

Kis-ack's handsome face became dark with rage as he learned what had happened to his father and of the treatment meted out to the dead body—the kind of treatment normally reserved for the lowest criminal. How dare they do this to his father, son of a chief and husband of a chief's daughter!

From that day on Kis-ack could think of nothing except how he could kill the Stoneheads for what they had done to his father, and for the heartache they had caused to his kind and gentle mother. At last he understood why they had been forced to live hidden away for all these years.

But each time he prepared to go and attack the Stoneheads, his mother would say, "Wait. When I have finished your magic coat, then you will be safe."

And day by day she went on sewing the bird skins

together with tiny stitches. It took many, many days to complete. The coat was at last finished, and as she held it out for Kis-ack to put on, she smiled, saying, "Now I shall not lose you as I lost your father. The dream I have dreamed so long will now come true."

"Along with all my magic, how will this coat help me?" Kis-ack asked.

"Climb to the top of the waterfall, and then jump," was the answer she gave him. He did as he was told; he leapt into the air, and found himself gliding, to land lightly beside his mother.

"Now, my son, the waiting is over. You can safely avenge your father's death."

The next night a full moon rose above the Saanich hills, a big red disk hanging in the sky, flooding the land with a soft glow and turning night into a summer dawn. Kis-ack, dressed in his bird coat, made his way along the slope of Mount Tzouhalem. Following his mother's directions, he reached a ledge overlooking the Stonehead village.

He heard shouts. House-high boulders, dressed in fern-covered moss, stood sentinel. In an open field below him, the hated Stoneheads were playing an ancient game with a spherical object made of reeds plaited and woven into the shape of a football. Though he never doubted his mother's word, he found it difficult to believe that a people could be as repulsive as she had described. They looked brutal, with round hairless heads. Their actions were equally uncouth. As they raced across the field, they kicked indiscriminately at the ball or at anyone within reach. He watched as one of the players was viciously kicked and fell to the ground, unconscious. The game continued and no one stopped to help him.

Kis-ack gave a resounding cry, spread his arms, and leapt from the ledge to glide over the Stoneheads and land on a mound a hundred feet away. The young Stoneheads stood paralysed; this apparition was outside their experience.

Another mighty leap, and Kis-ack sailed over them again, taunting, "Are you the great Stoneheads? Are you fearless warriors or a herd of timid deer? Send out your braves!"

No one stayed to face him. Instead they fled to the shelter of the longhouse to tell the elders about the flying bird-man who had suddenly appeared to mock them.

"Are you afraid of a bird?" the councilmen laughed. One old man shook his head, saying, "Too bad; if they are so cowardly perhaps they should go and sit with the women. Even they could protect them from this bird!"

When Kis-ack returned home, he told his mother how well her magic coat had carried him, and how the Stoneheads had run, stumbling over each other in the rush to get away. She listened in silence as he spoke of his plan to get rid of the Stoneheads, but she was afraid for her son's overconfidence in his success. She reminded him again of their great cruelty and of their unnatural ability to withstand every weapon that had been brought against them, a gift that had given them the name of Stoneheads.

But the young man was now even more convinced

that the time had come to avenge his father's murder and to rid the tribes of these monsters. All that was needed was a weapon sufficiently strong to overcome their unique capacity to withstand attacks from any kind of club or spear that had so far been used against them.

Next morning Kis-ack went into the forest. Using his stone axe, he cut a limb from an oak tree. Then, locating a hard rock, he brought the bough crashing down on it with all his strength, and the wood splintered into fragments. Next he tested a branch from a wild crab tree, but the same thing happened. His heart was heavy; would he ever find a wood sufficiently tough to crush the impenetrable skulls of the evil Stoneheads?

Then he saw a yew tree growing from the side of the mountain. Climbing, he cut off a branch and again tested it with a powerful blow, and this time it was the rock that split into a thousand pieces. The yew was, in fact, so hard that it took him the rest of the day to sever two more limbs, from which he would fashion clubs. Well seasoned, they could be used as weapons to exterminate his father's murderers.

When the clubs were ready for his coming encounter, Kis-ack fastened on his coat of many wings and, half walking, half flying, he returned to the cliff above the Stoneheads' encampment. When he arrived, he saw that the young bucks were out in the clearing practising with bows and arrows, shooting through a hoop made of reeds thrown high in the air. The hills echoed with their yells and laughter. When one of them succeeded in shooting several arrows through the flying circle, he cried,

"Come again, bird-man, come again, my aim is true."

Responding to the challenge, Kis-ack leapt into the air. Gliding past the bewildered braves, he struck the heads of three with his yew club, and they shattered like slate. Another leap, and more were killed. Those too astonished to run were clubbed on the spot. Following the rest into the village, he smote them all. Not one did he spare. With each blow his heart rejoiced as he shouted, "Kopa nika papa (for my father)."

One single warrior was able to recover sufficiently to stand and try to shoot Kis-ack down, but when he saw his arrow swerve in flight, deflected as if by some magic shield, he dropped his bow and plunged into the river. Breathing through a reed, he remained submerged until the bird-man, with a final cry of victory, left the village.

When it was dark, the sole survivor crept ashore and found all his people dead. Running to the beach, he took one of the light one-man canoes and paddled furiously until he reached Nanaimo, where another tribe took him in. He told the story as many times as there were days left for him to live, and that was a great many, for he died of old age, the last of the savage Stoneheads.

Kis-ack and his mother took possession of the Khenipsen village and Kis-ack became a mighty chief, much loved and respected by other tribes.

Word of Kis-ack's vengeance travelled swiftly. Indian bands came from near and far to pay homage to the brave man who had freed them from the hated Stoneheads. They brought gifts of blankets, furs, and the loveliest of their maidens. They came to honour Kis-ack's mother, too, for it was her wisdom and training that had made it possible for one man to accomplish what complete tribes had long wanted: to bring an end to Stonehead rule and peace to the Cowichan Valley.

A great potlatch was given in celebration. Once more the nights were filled with the sound of singing. Drumbeats told a tale of joy and gratitude, for the Cowichan tribes could now live in harmony without fear of their neighbours.

———

When Danny had finished speaking, we sat in silence. He had travelled far back in time, and I was trying to absorb all he had told me, feeling honoured to have shared this experience with him. At last I asked, "Is it possible that what happened in the past can sometime come back again? My sister Edie and I have heard and seen many strange things since we have lived here at Green Point."

"You too?" he questioned.

"Yes, and several friends who have visited with us have experienced the same things."

"I think perhaps you have the power that we people have. Maybe sometimes my people hear things that happened a long, long time ago, just like it was happening now." He paused, looking into space, and then continued, "Some of us can hear the old people singing and the sound of drums—like it used to be. Some people can hear the sounds of the old days come back—not many, but some do. Maybe it comes to you!"

Danny pointed to our left, across the water in the direction of Saanich, waited a moment, and then continued,

"Some night, when the big red moon comes up over there and puts out the light of the stars, you lie down on the earth near the water and you listen. Then maybe you hear Kis-ack fighting and the drums beating, and the singing. Just like it happened, right here where my people live now."

Danny Thomas was right. Several years had passed and a group of us were camping overnight at Separation Point. It was the time of year when great schools of spring salmon pass through Sansum Narrows, swimming close to shore and skirting around the Point to enter Cowichan Bay, heading for the mouth of the river. It was our plan to be out on the water, fishing lines trailing, when night gave way to the first grey light of dawn.

We made camp around a driftwood fire and prepared our supper on the little beach near the end of the Point. I can't remember all who made up the group, except that my sister Edie and my young daughter Carol were in the party.

There was a lot of light-hearted joshing going on as we all made sure our tackle was in order and chose our favourite lures. Bets were made as to who would catch the first, the largest, and the most fish. When all was ready for a quick start in the morning, we scooped hollows in the pebble beach to fit hips and shoulders of bodies accustomed to soft beds and, sliding into our sleeping bags, we settled down for the night.

It was quite late when I was awakened by the sound of beating drums. Everyone else appeared to be asleep, as no one moved or said a word. In a short while I heard voices joining the rhythmic throbbing of the drums, the sounds sometimes swelling in volume as though quite close, at other times becoming fainter and further away.

My daughter, who was next to me, suddenly said, "What is that?" Then my sister sat up and said, "It's an Indian dance—but they don't have their dances at this time of the year. And anyway, they're all away hop picking."

She was quite right. It was the time of year when all the Indian villages were deserted, the inhabitants away in Washington State picking hops or gathering crops wherever extra hands were needed. It was also the time of the harvest moon. There it was, hanging in a cloudless sky above the Saanich hills, a large, orange-red plate, so bright it did, in fact, put out the lights of the stars.

The strange part was that none of the others with us could hear a thing—though everyone was wide awake by now—even though to the three of us the sound was as distinct and as real as though a dance was in progress just around the Point.

I have often wondered, had I camped there again, would I have heard the Stoneheads' war cries or the crash of breaking stones, the way it sounded when Kis-ack shattered their skulls and ended the Stoneheads' rule of might and terror? I regret to say I never had an opportunity to find out, but perhaps, to quote old Danny, "Somebody, sometime, will hear 'em—not many, but some will."

I only hope that someone does, some day, hear the sounds of Kis-ack's battle which brought peace to those who now live on these tranquil shores, and that they will honour the brave man and his wise mother who made it all possible.

Johnny Page leaving Green Point, heading home after telling the legend of "Red Eye, White Eye."

Johnny Page

It had been an extremely dry summer, and the Cowichan River was reduced to a shallow trickle where it flowed past the cottage where Mother and I were living at Green Point. At high tide the sea would sweep in to a depth of several feet, completely covering the flats which extended up to and beyond the village of Khenipsen, where Rosalie Seletze', Danny Thomas, and Johnny Page lived.

Johnny was the last of the Natives to make friends with us. The breakthrough came around eight o'clock one morning. Mother and I were having our first cup of tea when we heard a knock on the door. I opened it and saw Johnny standing there, cap in hand. Without looking at me, he said, "My canoe—I can't get up river—I leave it here; when tide come back, I get it then?"

"But of course you may. We are having a cup of tea. Come in and have one."

He hesitated, then stepped inside, saying, "Tea, ah, that would be good."

After three cups of tea and much talk, mostly from Mother about fishing and what luck he'd had that morning, Johnny un-

bent to the point of being almost friendly. As he left to walk the half-mile home, Mother said, "Anytime you can't get up the river, tie your canoe here—you are always welcome."

And so began the friendship with the last holdout in the village. From then on, through the long, dry summer of 1929, Johnny often left his canoe tied at the point; sometimes he would slip away unobserved, other times we would see him and ask him in for a cup of tea.

One morning when Mother had just finished cooking a mouth-watering breakfast of bacon and eggs, hash brown potatoes, and oven toast to be spread with homemade jelly, we saw Johnny tie his canoe and start to head home.

I called out, "Good morning! Any luck?"

"No, no fish."

"We are just going to have breakfast—come in and join us—you must be hungry after fishing since dawn."

When, somewhat to our surprise, he accepted, we could now be sure that the ice was broken.

When we had eaten, Johnny and I went outside and sat on the beach, watching three bald eagles circling overhead, soaring effortlessly. After a while, I turned to him, saying, "How I wish I could rise high in the sky and look down, as they do."

Johnny said, "There is a legend of a young brave who reached beyond the sky and walked with and talked to the people living there."

"Would you tell me about it?" I asked. "I do so much want to learn about your legends."

After a pause, he responded, "I will tell you the story of Red Eye and White Eye." I was delighted, and listened spellbound as his narrative unfolded.

The Legend of Red Eye and White Eye

as told by Johnny Page

It happened a long, long time ago, when the world was smaller, and the sky was not so far away. Two young brothers, the older just turned eighteen and the younger nearly seventeen, would sit on the beach at Cowichan Bay and wonder about the two large holes in the heavens. There were also many small holes in the sky, but these two big ones twinkled as though they were winking at them.

The younger asked his older brother, "Do you think there are people up there, looking down on us?"

"Just what I have been wondering. I have named those two Red Eye and White Eye, and I think they belong to two girls who wish to meet us."

"But how could we get up there?" the younger questioned. "I know you are the best runner and swimmer and the strongest of the braves—but not even you could jump that high."

The older brother smiled as he asked, "Who can make an arrow fly straighter? Who can shoot truer, and who in this land can send an arrow as far?"

"No one," was the reply.

"Now, little brother, I shall tell you what I have

planned. On the night when the new sliver of moon appears in the sky, have your canoe ready. I shall need you to paddle me to the centre of the bay. You must hold the canoe steady when I stand up and shoot my arrows, one into the other, until they are anchored in the heavens. Then I shall climb until I reach that upper land."

The younger brother begged to be allowed to go with him, but the older brother explained to him why it wasn't possible, saying, "I shall want you to wait here, and come with your canoe if I need to return."

"But—how will I know if you are coming back?"

"You forget, I have a powerful voice. I shall cup my hands around one of the holes and shout 'Come!' so loud that all the dogs will bark and run around madly. They will wake the children, who will begin to cry; the mothers and fathers will get up, and soon the whole village will be awake. Then you will know it is time to come for me."

It was three weeks until the sliver of moon would rise again. The older brother worked by day and far into the night until he had made enough arrows to reach the sky. When all was ready, they stepped into the canoe, the older brother with his bow and bundles of arrows, and the disappointed younger brother paddling. They moved out to the centre of the bay until they were almost directly beneath Red Eye.

Luckily, it was a calm evening; no ripple disturbed the water. Then the older one stood up in the canoe and shot one arrow into another until they formed a link to the heavens, ending within his reach. Then, lifting himself up hand over hand, arrow after arrow, he disappeared from sight.

The courageous young man's climb ended within reach of a small hole which he managed to crawl through, and he found himself in a land much like his own, or so he thought at first. The people he saw looked much like himself, but the trees and birds were different.

He walked on until he met an old woman sitting beside the path he was taking. Then he stopped and asked, "I am a stranger here. Could you please point the way so that I may find Red Eye and White Eye?"

"Young man, go back to where you came from. You would have a dangerous journey ahead of you. Go back, I say, while you are still safe."

"Oh, wise mother, you must help me; tell me about the dangers ahead, so that I may escape from them."

The woman shook her head from side to side for a long time before she said, "You could be risking your life; but if you must go on, I shall give you three things to take with you. Maybe they will keep you safe." She reached into a pouch beside her and handed the young man a small bird skin, the same colour as the bark on the trees growing nearby. It looked much like a sparrow from home, except it had a long and very sharp beak. Next she gave him a baby octopus, and, lastly, a shell that looked something like a clam. He opened it and saw that it contained a fine, white powder.

"Thank you for your kindness, wise mother. Now would you tell me how a bird skin, an octopus, and this powder could protect me, and from what?"

"You are a stranger here. You do not know of the evil women who would trap you. She collects young men, and they are never seen again. If you should fall into her clutches, breathe a pinch of the powder, and you will become small enough to fit into the bird skin and fly away. Another pinch, and you will become yourself again."

She sat quietly, as if thinking deeply, before she added, "There is much danger you should be warned about, but I may not tell you. The powder holds magic—use it wisely and guard it well. If you throw it at someone, it will make a noise compared to which thunder would sound like the rumblings of a baby's belly, and you will see them no more. Be careful not to drop it."

"And the octopus? How will it help me?"

"Ah . . . " she said. "You want to find Red Eye and White Eye. They play in the lake during the day, but, when their father is asleep at night, they look down through their holes at the land below, watching the young men they have taken a fancy to."

The young brave stood quietly for a moment, saying to himself, "Yes, I was right—they are girls, and they wanted me to come here."

The old woman interrupted his thoughts as she said, "The little octopus—when you change into it, you will be able to swim in the water with those girls and that is how you will get to know them." She added, "I wish you well. Go on your way. Take the path to your left and you will see the lake where the girls play. But don't forget, I have warned you. Beware of the father, and above all, of Red Eye."

"Thank you again," the young man said, as he strode off down the path she had indicated. As he walked, he saw many things that were strange to him. A frog ran across his path instead of hopping as frogs did in his world. But he hadn't time to ponder these things, because when he looked ahead he saw a woman staring at him. She was pleasant looking and wore a friendly smile as she greeted him, saying, "I am so glad to see you, young man. I have dropped my magic ring and cannot find it. Would you help me look for it?"

Remembering how the old lady had gone out of her way to aid him, the young man was only too happy to return a favour. "Tell me what it looks like and where you think you lost it," he said, "and I shall do what I can to help you."

"Follow me, and I shall take you there. It is a bright ring with a stone which should be easy to see on the ground. My sight is dim, but with your young eyes I feel sure you will find it."

As she spoke, she led him into a forest. The trees were unlike any he had ever seen. Some were tall with blue foliage; others appeared to be dead, split open down the middle. It was to one of these that the woman led him. Pointing, she said, "I think the ring fell off my finger as I walked past, swinging my hand."

Without thinking, the young man stepped forward to look. As he scanned the ground within the hollow, the woman gave him a mighty shove, sending him headfirst into the heart of the tree. As he landed on hands and knees, he heard a loud "clank" as the cleft tree slammed shut, trapping him inside. He heard the woman's raucous laughter as she danced with glee at the young man's predicament, exulting, "I have caught many—how many I cannot remember. Now there is one less of those who would pass me by for younger women."

For a moment the young man was stunned and in shock, until he remembered the lucky charms he had been given. Opening the clam shell, he sniffed a little of the powder, and soon felt himself small enough to fit into the bird skin. He was thus able to fly up the hollow trunk, clutching the shell and the octopus in his claws, until he saw a glimmer of light coming through a hole where once a limb had grown. In a few minutes the bird's sharp beak had enlarged the knothole until it was big enough to fly through and escape.

And so he flew on, still in his disguise, until he came to a lake. There he saw the two girls standing up to their waists in the water, playfully splashing each other. Perched on a nearby tree the young man watched them for a while. Then he flitted to the ground, shed the bird skin, and slipped into the little octopus. (He was still small enough and so did not need the magic powder.)

Hiding the shell and the bird skin, he crawled down to the lake and swam to where the girls were playing, and listened to them talking. They were each as beautiful as the other, the older (whom he understood to be Red Eye) perhaps the prettier, though she sounded overly domineering as she said to her sister, "Stop this silly playing now. Come scrub my back with the reed sponge. And you be careful not to scratch me, or I will tell Father."

The younger girl, who, he decided, must be White Eye, hastened to do as she was told. But as she gently rubbed her sister's back, the young man, now swimming underwater in the octopus skin, began tickling White Eye's leg. She stopped what she was doing and, reaching down, caught the little creature and lifted him out of the water.

"Do look at this tiny thing, sister. Isn't it pretty; now I shall have a new pet."

"That ugly thing, throw it away!" the other girl ordered. "It is disgusting—kill it!"

"No, please, I want to keep it. Poor thing, it must be lonely."

"Throw it away—do as you are told, or I shall tell Father."

White Eye knew how angry her father would be if she disobeyed, so she put the tiny octopus back in the water and watched as it swam away.

When he reached the shore, the young man, still in the octopus skin, made his way to where he had hidden the magic powder. Opening the shell, he again sniffed a little of its contents, and at once resumed his normal shape and size. Placing his magic charms in a pouch he wore on a thong around his neck, he made his way around the shore of the lake in the direction of the sisters. He saw that they were now wrapped in some sort of soft, clinging mantle, the likes of which he had never seen before.

Not wishing to frighten them, he waited until they became aware of him. Only then did he speak, saying,

"I am a stranger in your land. I have come from another world to meet you."

Red Eye was the first to respond. As she approached him, she said, "You are welcome here. Come with us and I shall introduce you to my father. He will be glad to see you—oh yes, very glad."

The three of them climbed the path to the place where the sisters lived. On entering their home the young brave was greeted by a large man, overpowering in his presence, who fixed him with a commanding look, saying, "You are here to ask for the hand of my elder daughter—to that I agree."

"But no, asking your forgiveness, it is the younger that I would wish to share my life with."

The father gave a roar as he said, "No one, but I mean no one, shall have my younger daughter until the older one has her mate."

Red Eye smiled her agreement as she added, "My father is right. I have a special way that will be the end of all your seeking—do come and let me prove it to you."

The young man felt an instinctive shiver of fear run through him. But he was a brave man, and determined, so he answered, "It is this girl and none other I would have."

No one had ever stood up to Red Eye or to her father before, so they were immobilized with rage, giving the young man time to sweep White Eye under his arm and run out of the house with her. Red Eye quickly followed in close pursuit. Once outside the door, the young brave reached into his pouch and, drawing out the shell, he threw it through the entrance, where it blew apart the house, and all within it. The noise was indeed louder than any thunder—so loud, in fact, that the heavens shook. A cloud of black smoke darkened Red Eye's star for a while, and since that time it has shone with a dull, steady, red glow.

Meanwhile, the younger brother heard first the great thunder, and then his brother's voice calling, "Come!" As was foretold, the dogs, alarmed by the clamour, started to bark and run wildly, waking the children, whose crying woke their mothers and fathers, until there was no one, not even a bird, left asleep.

The younger brother, on hearing the agreed signal, jumped into his canoe and paddled furiously until he reached the arrow-chain hanging from the sky. His timing was right; his brother was already descending, arrow by arrow, and as he drew closer, the younger could see that his brother was bringing someone with him, clinging to his back with arms clasped around his neck.

And so the young brave and White Eye came safely home to earth at Cowichan Bay.

When the brothers looked into the heavens again, they saw that Red Eye and White Eye no longer twinkled. Red Eye now had a dull red glow, but White Eye was a clear evening star. They were the first stars to cease to flicker, and ever since then, they have shone with a steady light.

———

When Johnny finished telling the legend, we sat together on the beach for what seemed to me a very long time. I was full of questions, and yet did not wish to disturb his mood, for he appeared to be a long, long way away. The tide had come in and his canoe was afloat. He made a move to get up and leave, but I delayed his departure by asking, "Tell me what the kind old woman could not warn him against."

"I can't tell you that."

"Why not, Johnny? It is part of the legend—I need to know. Please tell me."

"Well, I tell you. It was good that the young man picked the younger sister; if he had mated with the older girl, she would have killed him, just like she had many who had chosen her before. In her woman's parts she had a pair of pincers, and if the young brave had mated with her—well, she would have unmanned him."

"But why?" I insisted. "Why didn't the old woman warn him?"

"She was afraid of the father. He had great powers and had trained even the birds to tell him what was being said or done in his land. Whoever disobeyed was killed. The old woman did not want to die, so she only told the young man as much as she could safely and survive."

Johnny ended up by saying, "I think we are all the same; wherever we come from, there is always someone bigger and stronger who can make us do things that we should not, or not do the things we should."

He stood up then, and I walked with him to his canoe. I held it as with great agility he climbed aboard and shoved off. He took hold of the oars and began rowing with a peculiar fin-like motion, heading for home.

I called after him, "I'll see you at dawn on the fishing

ground. Good luck and thank you for the legend." He lifted one hand from an oar in acknowledgement and continued on his way.

Johnny Page died on October 9, 1945, aged eighty. He is buried in St. Anne's Catholic churchyard on the Tzouhalem Road outside Duncan.

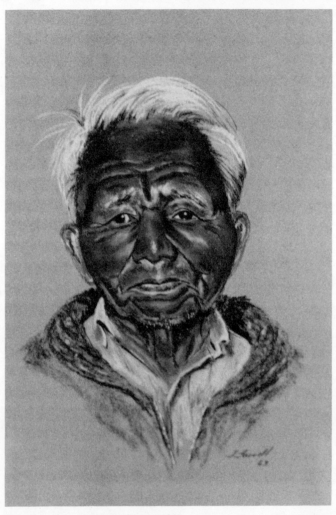

Sam Tom, from a portrait done in 1962.

Sam Tom

During my earlier association with the Native people of Vancouver Island in the 1920s, I heard talk of Sam Tom, a Salish Indian who lived in Mill Bay, and who was considered the most knowledgeable and the best raconteur of his people's legends, but it was not until the early 1960s that I was successful in arranging a meeting with him. This was accomplished through the good offices of Wilson Duff, at that time curator of anthropology at the Royal British Columbia Museum in Victoria.

I was, of course, delighted to have been given the opportunity to get to know this venerable figure. Naturally, I hoped to be able to persuade him to tell me one of the "old-time tales." The date was set for a few days ahead, a Friday, as I recollect, and my sister, Edie Cross, offered to drive me up-island for the interview.

When the day arrived, it proved anything but promising. The sky was darkly overcast with scudding, low-lying clouds threatening to spill over at any moment. Undaunted, Edie said, "Ready? Let's go." As we left home, the rain began to fall, and by the time we reached Goldstream Park, it was coming down in earnest. When we crested the Malahat, it was pelting so hard that the windshield wipers could hardly keep up with it.

Feeling guilty, I said, "Pull over to the verge and let's decide whether to go on or turn back." But Edie kept going, saying, "He's well up in his nineties, and his health is far from good; this may be our last chance." So, bless her, we continued on. Eventually we reached the turnoff to Mill Bay, and there to the right of the ferry dock we could see Sam's yellow cottage.

Edie parked the car, and we made a dash up the path to his door. When we knocked, a surprisingly strong voice called, "Come in!" We opened the door, and saw the old man lying on his bed, cosily ensconced under a colourful quilt. His flushed face was creased with wrinkles, but it was his deepset eyes that held my attention. They were so penetrating that I felt he could see right into my inner self. And then I caught a glimpse of humour, which spread to his smile as he said, "Well, you ladies sure picked a bad day to come to see me."

I apologized for the intrusion, suggesting that it might be better to visit another day if he didn't feel up to talking to us. "Ah no," he said, "you came through this rain to see me. Stay now; hang up your coats near the stove to dry and sit a while."

We did as he said, and when we were seated, he asked, "Are you from the museum?"

"No, we're not, although my sister Edie and I have both gone on digs with Wilson Duff. Edie's interest is in your people's art.

She has a wonderful collection of your artifacts, perhaps the largest and most important private collection in Canada."

"I have heard of you," Sam said to Edie. Then, looking back to me, he asked, "You want to write the old-time stories?"

"Very much so," I said. "When I was nineteen, Johnny Page and Danny Thomas told me a few, and we got to know the people at the Khenipsen village when we lived at Green Point in 1929. We had to drive through the village in order to reach our home, and we became friends."

"Ah yes, I knew them. Peter Jack was chief in those days."

He looked out the window, and was silent for a while; then he said, "You have a long, wet drive home; maybe I have time to tell you one story."

Edie and I sat quietly, waiting for Sam to begin. He seemed to withdraw into himself and speak as though we were not present. His memory, like his eyes, was like a clear mirror as he began reciting the legend of his people's beginnings in the Cowichan Valley. His expression, his gestures, and his choice of words painted a powerful picture of the traditional version of the beginnings of his tribe. Sam's English was only slightly broken, and, without attempting to imitate his speech, I shall write the story as nearly as possible in his own words.

He began, "This is the legend of See-la-tha, the first man to come to earth. It tells of Wauk-us, the first dog ever to be upon this land. It tells of the women who gave See-la-tha many children. It is the descendants of these children and their children's children down to the present day who now populate the Cowichan Valley."

The Legend of See-la-tha

as told by Sam Tom

A long, long time ago, so far back that no man can tell what year it was, the first man came to earth and made Cowichan his home.

When the Great Spirit (Saghalie-Tyee) saw this valley, he said, "There are birds of the land and those that swim upon the waters. So great are they in number that the sky turns any hour of the day into night when they take wing." He saw the beasts of the forest: the deer, the elk, the cougar, the large black bear, and the smaller brown bear. He saw the beaver, too, building the dams which form the shallow lakes and ponds around which the ducks (kweh-kweh) build their nests and linger until their young are big enough to fly. Only then would they leave these still, calm waters.

The Great Spirit saw all this and also the sheltered inlets reaching in from the sea, like fingers stretching from a giant's hand. And in Cowichan Bay he saw the salmon leaping in the air to elude the whale, the porpoise, the dogfish shark, and the seal, until they churned the waters white in their frenzied efforts to escape, first from one, then from the other.

Then the Great Spirit saw a lack, not of might or

number, but of a being which would bring a balance between the two. This being must have the one thing the
other life did not possess. So he made Man and gave him
a spirit and a mind, with the ability to learn and grow
wise. Because, although the creatures that lived in the
water and upon the land had instinct to guide them, and
intellect, they had no power to plan for the future.

So Man was made, smaller than the whale, but
equally that much bigger than the birds. Man did not
need great strength or fleetness to survive, for he had
knowledge, and that made him master of all other living things.

Thus was See-la-tha formed. The Great Spirit trained
him until he had learned all that he must know, and the
rules by which he must live. Then The Great Spirit said,
"Now you are ready to go to a new land."

"Will you take me there?"

"No, I shall let you down on a long rope," The Great
Spirit answered. "And when you touch the earth you
must undo the knot that holds you so that I may draw
the rope back into the Heavens."

"Shall I be the only man there?" See-la-tha asked.

"In time you will not be alone. But first you must
choose a place to live, and build yourself a home. Then
you are to find a mate, a woman, and she will give you
children and so populate the land."

With that, the Great Spirit tied the end of the rope
around See-la-tha and let him down from the sky, and
he descended at the foot of Mount Provost in the heart
of the Cowichan Valley.

See-la-tha undid the knot and watched the rope until it disappeared, then looked around him. He saw many deer grazing nearby. They were not in any way afraid of him, only curious about the strange being who had so suddenly appeared amongst them. He stayed for a while watching the dainty animals as they went back to nibbling the grass or frolicking in play. Then he left to explore more of the beautiful valley sloping gently away from him.

During his descent, See-la-tha had seen a broad, winding ribbon more blue than the sky, sparkling in the sun to the northeast of where he had landed. He set out to find this jewel. He first followed a small stream which led him to the shores of a beautiful lake. This was Quamichan. He stood by its waters and let his eyes sweep around the oval shoreline. Across the lake he saw a large herd of elk browsing on the lush grass, taking cover from the noonday sun beneath stately poplar trees. Further back grew enormous oak and maple trees, dotted here and there as though granting each other just the right amount of space in which to grow.

Higher up the side of Mount Tzouhalem was the deep blue-green of majestic firs, standing guard and giving shelter to all in need beneath their overlaying branches.

To the right of where See-la-tha stood was a miniature island nestling in the lake, surrounded by bulrushes and crowned with lacy greenery. In the days to come he would learn that loons nested there, and in the dark of night their haunting cries would chill his heart and cause him to ache with loneliness.

Still eager to find the jewel-like ribbon of water that he had seen on his descent from the heavens, See-la-tha set out from the shore of the lake. Before long he came to the Cowichan River, which he immediately recognized as the shining object he had been seeking.

Squatting on the moss-covered bank, he watched the water flowing past, and in it saw many silvery objects darting about, swimming hard against the current. Some rested a while, nosed in behind smooth boulders, while others, undaunted, swam on.

These steelhead and rainbow trout were to become his most ready supply of food. In the fall, he would find the river an undulating mass of swirling black and silver bodies, as countless thousands of spring and coho salmon headed upstream seeking their place of birth, there to spawn—and die.

On this bend of the river, safe above the highest mark of floodwater, See-la-tha decided to build his home. He named the place Quamichan. There were cedar trees of all sizes growing along the bank. From them he could cut and split planks to build himself a house, where he would live warm and safe from any of the four-legged animals he had seen. Everything he would need was at hand.

Having made his plans for the busy days ahead, he satisfied his hunger that evening by feasting on brambleberries, which grew nearby in profusion.

As the last of the sunset faded, and the black velvet cloak of night lowered across the sky, See-la-tha stretched out on the mossy ledge above the river, where the heat of the sun had baked its warmth deep into the rock beneath, and he slept. In such a way did he spend his first night in the valley.

The new day was just breaking when he was awakened by something cold and damp sniffing at his feet. Then he felt breath upon his legs. Inwardly tensed and ready to spring, he remained motionless. Then slowly opening his eyes, he saw the strangest animal watching him. It wasn't a large animal. The body would only reach above his knees when standing beside him. It had hair like the wolf, and resembled one more closely than any other animal See-la-tha had seen, but in the middle of its head, slanting forward, grew a single, sharp-pointed horn about a hand's span in length. Its colour was also different from the wolf; instead of the mottled grey-brown fur, this animal had a white coat.

Sensing that it was friendly, See-la-tha remained quite still, whispering softly, "Come (Ha-mi)." At first the animal froze. Then it slowly turned around three times and, curling its body into a ball, it lay down beside him and licked his hand.

This was the beginning of the loyal friendship between man and dog, for such was this animal. His name was Wauk-us. When hunting, Wauk-us proved invaluable. He could trail anything that walked the land, just as he had trailed See-la-tha, and move so quietly that none suspected it was being followed. Cougars would climb a tree for safety at the sound of his bark, and even wolves would run from him. They feared with good reason, for with a sharp stab of his horn Wauk-us could kill.

The days passed quickly, too quickly. There were soon not enough daylight hours in which to accomplish all the tasks See-la-tha had set himself to do. The making of the most necessary tools and the building of his house did not take long, however, and soon he was snug and secure against all weather. Then other needs filled his days. There was game to be trapped for food and hides, and fish to be caught. In fishing, Wauk-us had more luck than See-la-tha. He would stand in the river, deftly hook a salmon on his horn, and toss it onto shore. Meanwhile, See-la-tha would try to catch fish in his hands. But often the slippery creatures would elude his grasp and with a flip of the tail swim away, almost as if they were laughing at him.

One day an especially big steelhead got away, so he and Wauk-us went to bed hungry that night. That was when See-la-tha decided to build a weir across the river. The splitting of cedar shakes and driving them into the riverbed with a hafted hammer, the gathering of cedar roots and twisting them into long sturdy ropes was an arduous task, but at last it was done, and he felt it would be strong enough to withstand the onslaught of the spring floods. He and Wauk-us could now have fish any time.

As the season changed, he worked late into the night by the light of the fire, making knives and spears by rubbing slate against sandstone, and chipping flints to make arrowheads. See-la-tha was so busy that he had no time to feel lonely. But at last everything was in readiness for the coming winter. When the days grew shorter, he spent more and more time inside his house, sitting beside the fire that burned so brightly on the stone hearth in the centre of his home. Now he began to feel a great loneliness within himself.

One night, as he lay on his primitive pallet, he watched the smoke lazily rise to escape through the square hole in the roof. As he looked on, the smoke began to take form and a figure stood out clearly. Gradually he recognized that it was a human figure, that of a woman. Then See-la-tha heard again the words the Great Spirit had said to him before he came to earth: "You are to find a mate and populate the land."

Unable to move or speak, he observed the woman floating before him. Her skin was the same burnished copper as his own, but hers was a lighter tone, and her hair, which flowed around her, had a silken sheen and was as dark and gleaming as the midnight waters of the river. Everything about the woman was new and strange to him. As he reached out his hand to touch her, the smoke gathered and hid her from view, then rose straight up and disappeared through the opening, taking the woman with it.

See-la-tha jumped to his feet and called, "Come back. Come back!" But there was no answer. He ran outside searching, but she was nowhere to be seen. He called again and again in a voice grown mighty with longing, but he got no answer. The only sound was the childlike cry of the cougar and, wafting on the still night air, the haunting cry of a loon, echoing his loneliness. See-la-tha was once again alone in the stillness beneath the empty, star-studded sky.

Remembering all the things he had been taught, and recalling the Great Spirit's promise that in time he would find a mate, See-la-tha thought, "Now I have been shown the likeness of a woman—surely this is a sign that I must fashion her with my own hands. Tomorrow I shall collect what I shall need in order to create her."

Having reached this conclusion, he was no longer troubled as he re-entered his house. That night he slept soundly, firm in the knowledge that he would soon have his promised companion, and so need never be lonely again.

See-la-tha, having had the vision of a woman, now knew what he must do. He had the knowledge of what she looked like, so he could now shape her likeness. Sunrise found him well on his way through the forest, a large deerskin pouch hanging limply from his arm and Wauk-us beside him. He knew that the female he had seen the night before had been a vision, and that she had been sent to him in that way so that he could mould a body in her likeness. But how?

Then he remembered that when hunting some months ago he had come upon an ancient oak, which had fallen and had been lying on the ground for many years. The wood was rotted and soft, and had crumbled at his touch. With this he would build the body of his companion.

When he reached the tree, he filled his pouch with

enough of the spongy substance to form the body of his vision. Next he searched for and collected the life-giving herbs that grew along the riverbank and under the trees. Once home, See-la-tha mixed the things he had gathered together, and moulded the shape of the woman. Finally, he rubbed more herb mixture onto the finished work. So well had he fashioned her that there were no joins to be seen, and her skin looked and felt just like his own. His little woman appeared very much alive. Placing her by the fire to warm and hasten the action of the herbs, he sat many hours each day, talking and encouraging her to respond.

"How good it will be to come home and find you waiting for me," he said, setting her in a more comfortable position.

She opened her eyes and looked at him.

See-la-tha's delight was a joy to see as he said, "Soon you will be really alive, and how good it will be to come home after a day's hunting, to find a warm house and dinner awaiting me." She nodded her head, and he laughed with happiness. Now he had someone to talk to and share his thoughts with.

"I have spent so much time with you that we are almost out of food," See-la-tha explained. "Tomorrow I must go hunting." Again she nodded her head, and this time she smiled her understanding.

Early next morning See-la-tha put some smoked salmon in his pouch and, placing some more within the woman's reach, said, "Eat, so that you grow strong. I may be gone for several days. Will you be alright?"

She rolled her eyes and again nodded her head, smiling.

"You have come alive so quickly!" See-la-tha told her as he put some dried leaves and grass beside her. "I expect to find you have made a basket with these when I return."

Once more she nodded.

"Here is enough wood to keep the fire going. Make sure it does not go out." So saying, he left.

Soon, he was deep in the forest, Wauk-us beside him. The fallen leaves were brown and crisp underfoot as he passed beneath a grove of maple trees with their bare branches spreading stark and clean in silhouette against the blue, sun-swept sky. Those trees in the dark depths of the ravine were hung with long streamers of yellow-green moss, like tattered sleeves on their gnarled old arms. See-la-tha carried his bow and arrow over his shoulder. In his right hand he held his sharpest spear, ready for instant action.

By the time he reached the shores of Shawnigan Lake it was sundown. He had already killed a deer and a cougar, which he placed in the forked branches of trees, high off the ground and safe from prowling wolves and other flesh-eaters. It had been a long day, and he was tired. He made a fire near the lake, for the night was cold. He shared his salmon with Wauk-us, then they lay down within the fire's glow, and slept until sunup.

***

Now it happened that two young maids, sisters, who lived at Sooke, had gone to the lake to gather reeds. The older sister noticed a faint line of smoke rising through the trees around a bend in the shoreline. Motioning her sister to be quiet, she said, "Who is it that makes fires? No one lives here."

"Fire does not come alone this time of the year," her sister replied.

"Come, we will go and see. Keep well hidden."

Overcome with curiosity, they crept through the woods until they could look down upon the fire. The girls watched See-la-tha as he ate a feast of lake trout.

"How handsome he is!" the elder sister whispered. "Let's follow and find out where he lives."

Just then the man gave a shrill whistle, and Wauk-us ran to him. The girls were amazed by the strange animal, who, obviously devoted to the man, leapt up and down in excitement while his tail wagged so fast it made his whole body shake from side to side.

The man said, "Sit!" and the dog at once became quiet and sat down, waiting until his master had put out the fire. Then the two headed back into the brush.

The girls trailed at a safe distance, keeping well hidden when See-la-tha stopped to skin the cougar, and again when he collected the deer.

"See how strong he is, little sister. That is a large buck, yet he walks as though he carries nothing."

"Don't talk. That animal keeps looking this way. It may have heard you."

They let a greater distance separate them before they

took up the trail again, and at last they came within sight of the Cowichan River, and there they saw See-la-tha enter his house.

Not knowing what to expect, the sisters hid behind a large tree growing beside the house and waited.

They hadn't long to wait, for suddenly they heard the man say in a loud, angry tone, "You lazy woman. You have done nothing. You worthless woman. If you could eat, why couldn't you put some wood on the fire?"

There was silence for a while, then smoke began to show.

"He's got the fire going," said the elder sister, pointing to the roof.

"His woman must be scared of him. She doesn't answer back."

The sisters giggled with hands over their mouths to muffle the sound. Then the elder said, her eyes all round and twinkling, "Shhh, any man as angry as he with his useless woman ... we could easily win him away for ourselves."

"Don't you shake your head at me," the girls heard him shout. "You haven't moved since I left. You lazy woman—you didn't even attempt to make a basket."

He strode out of the house, stopped, and called over his shoulder, "You keep that fire going. I'll bring you the deer ribs to roast. I am hungry, I tell you, and I want good food."

In a short time the girls heard him talking again.

"There! Now cook this while I clean the hides. I'll be

back by the time it is ready."

"It's safe now, little one. I can see him down by the river, scraping the fat from the skins. Let's go and take a peep inside."

"What about the woman? She will tell him."

"A woman who doesn't speak up to defend herself? She doesn't frighten me. Come on."

They crept around the house and, entering, saw the woman sitting by the fire, not moving, just staring at them.

She still didn't move when they went up to her. They asked her, "What's the matter? Aren't you going to cook the meat?"

Still the woman didn't speak; she merely shook her head and rolled her eyes.

"Help me take her outside, sister. We will hide her and do all the things she was supposed to do for him."

They carried her out and put her on the roof, and then hurried inside to carry out their plan.

"Keep a sharp lookout," the younger one warned. "We don't want the man to catch us."

Smiling, they went to work and soon had the house in order and the meat browning nicely on the spit above the glowing fire. Lastly, they wove a basket. Their nimble fingers soon completed a beautiful one from the reeds and grass the man had left for the woman. They laughed as they ran to their hiding place and waited for See-la-tha to return.

When he entered the house and they heard his cry of surprise, it was all they could do to keep from laughing out loud. They heard his deep voice call, "Where are you? Come back, you are a good woman. Come back and I'll never call you lazy again."

But of course there was no answer.

See-la-tha went outside, calling to the woman again and again, but the only sound he heard was the wind in the wings of a raven flying overhead.

Back in the house, Wauk-us was behaving in a very strange manner. Instead of sitting by the fire as he usually did when meat was cooking, his nose twitching in anticipation, he was rushing about, sniffing everything in the room. Then he jumped through the door, barking, and ran out just as See-la-tha saw the woman lying on the roof.

"What are you doing up there? How did you get there?" he asked in amazement, as he lifted her down and carried her back inside.

The girls could hear him talking, but so softly now that they could not make out what he was saying.

And so the night passed. In the morning, when the man and his strange animal went down to the weir to repair a weakened section, the sisters wasted no time in carrying out the last of their plans. Building a large fire where it could not be seen by See-la-tha, they stood by until the flames were leaping high. Then they ran and carried the woman to the bonfire and threw her into the heart of the flames.

There was one long, high-pitched scream before her body burst into flames and was swiftly reduced to ashes.

Then they proceeded to clean the house, fluffed up the skins of See-la-tha's bed, and started another meal cooking over a well-banked fire before returning to their hiding place.

See-la-tha was a very happy man when he got home and found all his needs taken care of. He was also a puzzled man. Once more, the woman was nowhere to be seen.

"Where are you hiding?" he called. "Wauk-us, go find her." The dog leapt outside, barking for See-la-tha to follow. He quickly showed his master where the girls were hiding.

Realizing they were discovered, the elder girl gave a sudden push that sent her sister flying into See-la-tha's arms. So great was his surprise that he just stood and held her, looking down at her lovely face, half hidden by her long, blue-black tresses.

"Little woman (Sle-mi)," he whispered. "I thank the Great Spirit. No longer shall I know loneliness. You have come, and you are real."

The elder girl came forward when she saw how delighted See-la-tha was to welcome her sister. She told him who they were.

Later, as the three of them sat around the fire in See-la-tha's home, first one and then the other girl spoke shyly of how they had tricked him. There was no laughter now, for it would not be fitting. Besides, they were afraid he might be angry with them for burning the woman he had made. After all, he must have worked long hours to build her, and she had developed to the state where she would have been really alive, even though her spirit could only be that of the trees, and her mind hard and as unbending as an oak.

See-la-tha listened, occasionally breaking a long silence by telling them about his life on earth. When all was said, the girls sat quietly with downcast eyes, not looking at See-la-tha, just waiting.

He, too, was silent, looking very solemn for a long, long time. At last he said, "It is well. Yes," he repeated, smiling at them, "it is well."

As for Wauk-us, he was very put out. No longer could he curl up to sleep with See-la-tha as was his wont, and naturally he felt jealous and neglected. It was quite some time before he made friends with the women, although he instantly took on the task of protecting the children as they were born.

Being neglected so often, Wauk-us took to wandering away from home, and one day he met and made friends with Stkeya, the she-wolf. Eventually they mated, and, strangely enough, not one of his descendants ever grew a horn.

In time, several of the pups returned with Wauk-us and became domesticated, but their wild mother could not be persuaded to venture close to the encampment, and kept well back from the sight and scent of humans. Sometimes, in the quiet of the night, when the moon rose above the hills to begin its journey across the vast, star-studded sky, those in See-la-tha's house would hear the distant, sharp yelp of a wolf, ending in a long drawn-out howl, and they would turn in their sleep.

Wauk-us, responding to the call, would order the excited pups to stay, and then steal away and race joyfully up the ridge to greet his mate.

Sam Tom died shortly after our visit, on February 9, 1965, at the age of 104. He is buried in the Malahat burial ground.

Abner Thorne, a councilman and elder of the Cowichan Band. Photographed at age 30 (circa 1954).

Agnes Thorne

In January 1992, my good friend Linda Vanden Berg, who shares my keen interest in Native folklore, drove me up-island to visit with Abner Thorne, an elder and councilman of the Cowichan Band, who, she believed, would be of great help to me in transcribing Salish words. Moreover, Abner's mother Agnes, who at eighty-five spoke little English but was fluent in her native Salish, was a gold mine as far as the old-time stories were concerned. Agnes' Salish name was Snook-nee-kwal-wet.

Abner's paternal great-grandfather, a Mr. Woodgate, jumped ship in Esquimalt from a British gunboat, married a Native woman, and changed his name to Thorne to avoid pursuit by the British Admiralty. He died in 1860. His son, Bill Thorne, owned two 34-foot dugout canoes, which he used to take thrill-seeking passengers from Lake Cowichan down through the rapids of the Cowichan River to Cowichan Bay, a forerunner of present-day whitewater rafting.

One of the first things that Abner said to me when we

met was, "I don't mind telling you these legends now. Older people know them, but when they die there's no record of them—their children don't know the stories, and it is important that they should be preserved and used by the education people in their Native Indian studies."

When Abner asked his mother to tell us about the origin of some of the landmarks along the coast of Vancouver Island and of the dangerous whirlpools of Sansum Narrows, this is the story she told.

Canoeing down the Cowichan River with Bill Thorne (Abner's grandfather) in one of Bill Thorne's 34-foot dugouts. A trip we took three times and I shall never forget the beauty nor the thrill of it. When Bill died, the canoes disappeared and so ended the "River Trips" (circa 1929). Left to right: Able Joe, Dolby Turner, Capt. H. Stuart Pearson, Bill Taylor.

The Monster of Octopus Point

as told by Agnes Thorne

I f you travel by boat from Maple Bay, on your right you will pass a large boulder called Paddy's Milestone. Carry on for another mile, and you will reach Octopus Point. It is here that the Sansum Narrows begin and where the supernatural being, Shuh-shu-cum (Open Mouth) used to lie at the tip of the Point with his snout out of the water. Should anyone try to pass, Shuh-shu-cum would open his mouth and suck in a huge gulp of water, the canoe, traveller, and all.

Those canoes that ventured too close to the Point were never seen again. This became a matter of great worry and concern to the villagers. The elders held meetings, asking questions and seeking advice as to what could be done. A few suggestions were forthcoming, but none seemed to be the solution to the problem.

At last the chief asked, "Is there no one who can rid us of this peril?"

All present shook their heads in bewilderment, except for the chief's eldest son, who said, "Let me try. I am not afraid. Who knows, perhaps I could make an end to this evil thing."

The gathering answered as one, "No, not you—we

have lost too many—not you."

The chief thanked the villagers for their concern for his son, adding, "I think that only a person of supernatural strength and wisdom could find a way to rid us of this demon."

The people listened in rapt attention as he continued, "I say let us send our best runners in all directions, from the rising to the setting sun, until one of them finds that person who shall rid us of this thing that swallows up our people."

So the fastest runners took off, some heading up-island, others to the south and west. The rest of the villagers waited. But one brave had another plan. He had heard of a man called Sum-ul-quatz who lived on the mainland, on the coast at a place now called Point Roberts. Sum-ul-quatz was said to have the strength of a thousand men. The young brave had decided that he, and only he, was the one to put an end to the monster and make the waters safe again.

Placing some food and water in his canoe, he paddled away from Maple Bay, giving a wide berth to Octopus Point. He beached his canoe in Burgoyne Bay on Saltspring Island. From there he climbed up and over Mount Maxwell, and continued across the island until he reached the southernmost harbour. A friend who lived there lent him a canoe, and he set out for the Strait of Georgia. Making his way between the islands, the young brave continued without stopping until he reached the mainland and made his way to Point Roberts.

Although overtired, the young brave at once began

his search for Sum-ul-quatz. This did not take long, for the man he sought was well known to everyone. Having found him, the young brave explained how the monster Shuh-shu-cum had become such a great menace to his people. He told of how they could not pass through Sansum Narrows to reach Cowichan Bay. He ended his story by saying, "My village is loud with the sound of wailing from the many wives and mothers who have lost their men."

When the young man had finished speaking, Sum-ul-quatz replied, "This is a very sad thing you tell me." He watched as the young messenger bowed his head low with exhaustion, unable to continue.

Sensing the deep anguish within the young man, Sum-ul-quatz took him by the arm, saying, "Come with me. I think I may be able to help you."

Leading the way to a long, shallow beach on which there were many large boulders, Sum-ul-quatz unwound the sash from his body, and without apparent effort picked up a boulder and placed it in the centre of the cloth. Then, using the sash as a sling, and much to the young man's astonishment, he swung it around his head several times and let fly.

The boulder soared up high into the sky, and was lost to sight. That one landed in Ladysmith, where it remains to this day.

Sum-ul-quatz chose another large stone and reloaded his huge sling. On the second try, the boulder landed near Mayne Island, just inside Active Pass. If you come from Vancouver on the ferry, you will see where it landed at the end of the first point after you enter the Pass.

The third shot went to Maple Bay and is still there at the end of Paddy's Point.

Having made these three unsuccessful attempts, Sum-ul-quatz explained, "I cannot aim properly; Mount Maxwell is too high and in the direct line of my shot. Wait a while and I shall ask him to crouch down."

And so he called to the mountain's spirit, asking him to hunch down and so give him a clear shot at Shuh-shu-cum. The spirit of the mountain was only too happy to do as he was asked, for he had seen so many good men sucked to their death by Shuh-shu-cum.

And so the top of Mount Maxwell lay down on its belly, its shoulders humped up and its head drawn in. Sum-ul-quatz picked up another boulder, aimed again, and this one passed clean over Mount Maxwell and hit Shuh-shu-cum right on his snout, shattering it and so putting an end to the ability of the monster to control the waterway of Sansum Narrows.

But Shuh-shu-cum was not completely destroyed. A part of him still lurks in those deep waters, but without his snout he can no longer suck people in. He can still make his presence felt, however. When he does, you will know he is nearby because of the great whirlpools which plague these waters.

Although the monster is no longer a direct threat to human lives, caution is still needed to avoid the swirls and eddies that occur when he shows his resentment by churning up the waters where he used to reign supreme.

But with care, canoes can now travel through the Sansum Narrows and return to their homes in safety.

If you should travel to Maple Bay, stand on the shore and look across the water. There you will see the great boulder that rests on a bed of shattered rock, now known as Paddy's Milestone. Octopus Point cannot be seen from here, but raise your eyes, and you will see that Mount Maxwell is still hunkered down in the position it assumed at Sum-ul-quatz's request.

The boulder that crushed the Monster's snout levelled Octopus Point before rolling away into the deep water, leaving the point looking as it does today.

Epilogue

It has taken me several years to trace the descendants of my old friends Rosalie and Johnnie Seletze', and it was not until January of this year that I was able to make contact with Mrs D. D. Dohn of the Indian Health Services in Duncan, who told me that Mary Johnnie, Rosalie's granddaughter, had recently retired from those services and was living in Duncan. I also learned that there was a grandson, Raphael Johnnie, who lived with his wife Maria at Khenipsen where his grandparents used to have their home.

I had been wanting to complete the story of the Khenipsen Natives and their legends for more years than I wish to admit, so it was with great excitement and some misgivings that I phoned Raphael. It would have been no surprise if his response to a total stranger had been cool, but to my delight I was invited to come to his house the following Sunday and meet his family.

Friends drove me to the Cowichan Valley, and I revisited the Khenipsen Village for the first time since I left Green Point in 1934.

We took the Tzouhalem Road, turned left onto the Khenipsen Road, and travelled what used to be a one-lane, deeply rutted dike, now widened into two lanes—and hard-topped! What a change from the 1930s, when I used to make my way along it in a Model T Ford after making sure that no one was about to attempt to do so from the other end!

Once past the dike, the now smooth road turned right, and I could vaguely discern the remains of Peter Jack's "city house," now a heap of fallen lumber surrounded by a tall thicket of plum trees. Beyond it, the longhouse had also collapsed, the only hint that it had ever existed being a stretch of flat ground, now covered with wild blackberry bushes.

To our right, the backwater still reflected the sky, but no canoes were to be seen, only six swans rippling the water as they glided majestically on their way, having taken over the sanctuary, moving as silently as the canoes once did when they headed to and from the fishing grounds each dawn and evening.

When we reached what had been the turnaround in the trail to where Rosalie and Johnnie's one-room cottage once stood, there was now a road leading up to the top of the knoll, so we drove uphill and stopped outside the new three-bedroom house where Raphael and Maria now live.

Maria was outside to greet us and usher us into the

living room. There, waiting for us, was Raphael, a tall man with a deep voice, and, as an added bonus for me, his son Delmar.

Ham and chicken sandwiches, plus cake and tea, were served by two sixteen-year-old boys. As we munched our food and sipped our tea, we talked of the old people and the old ways, but as we spoke, half of me was back in Rosalie's time. If only she could have been there, no longer having to wait for low tide to haul buckets of water from the river; no more coal oil lamps to fill or wicks to trim; no more trips to an outhouse, for there is now a bathroom, hot and cold running water, electricity, and television.

As I came back to the present, I asked Raphael if he knew of a good Salish artist who would be able to illustrate my work. Without hesitation he pointed to his son, Delmar.

"You are an artist?" I asked. Delmar indicated the many works of art around the room, saying, "I did those." His works are powerful. Much impressed, I asked, "Would you be interested in doing the illustrations for my book?"

"I would love to," he replied.

It is so right that Rosalie's great-grandson will add his spirit to my writings of the old people's legends of long ago.

The years have flown by, and everything has changed except for the warm welcome given me by the old people's descendants.

It is not often that one is allowed to step back into

the past. Time seemed to have stood still, and once again I felt accepted as a friend. Now I understand what Chief Dan George felt when he said: "My heart soars."

D.B.T.
Victoria, March 1992.

Delmar Johnnie Seletze', a member of the Khenipsen band, was born in 1946 and raised in Duncan. His work is not typical of Salish art, although he has studied with and learned from a variety of Salish artists. His art comes from the soul and is strongly influenced by the teachings of his grandparents and other elders, and by his dreams. Delmar studied first at Peninsula College of Art in Port Angeles, then at Malaspina College, where he developed an interest in printmaking, etching, and silkscreening.

Delmar Johnnie is a mystic. At a very young age, he often sat by the river near his home, where he watched and listened to an old man who sang a song while he cleaned fish. One day when Delmar sang this song, his grandmother asked where he had learned it. When he told her about the old man and the song, his grandmother identified the old man as her long-dead father and the song as his "thank you" song. Delmar was then given his great-grandfather's Native name, Seletze'. He now uses this name to identify his art and other significant life events.

Now a very active octogenarian, Dolby Bevan Turner spent her teenage years at Green Point on Cowichan Bay, Vancouver Island, where her immediate neighbours were the people of the Khenipsen Native band. As friendship and trust developed, she first heard some of the "old-time stories," sparking a lifelong interest in the legends, history, and culture of Canada's First Nations.

Though marriage, family, career, and sixty-five years intervened, Turner never gave up her quest to gather and preserve some of the stories that seemed otherwise destined to be forgotten. Careful always to respect the Native traditions, she waited until she could get the permission and approval of the elders of the band, some of whom have only recently come to realize that if these stories are not set down now, they are indeed in danger of being lost forever.

In When the Rains Came, *Dolby Turner writes eloquently about her friendship with the people of Khenipsen and profiles the elders who shared their stories with her.*